MR. HAPPY
and the Wizard
Roger Hargreaves

Original concept by
Roger Hargreaves

Written and illustrated by
Adam Hargreaves

EGMONT

Mr Happy goes to the Town Library every Saturday morning.

He went there last Saturday.

And he went there this Saturday.

He was looking along the shelves for a book to read when a very large and rather battered red volume caught his eye.

He pulled it out and looked at the spine.

It read, 'SPELL BOOK'.

He was about to return it to its place when a voice suddenly said, "Don't you dare! I've been stuck on that shelf for a week!"

Mr Happy dropped the book in surprise.

"Ow!" said the book, for it was the book that had spoken.

There was a face on the cover – nose, eyes, mouth, everything!

Mr Happy was too amazed to speak.

"Oooh," wheezed the book. "You get terribly cramped if you're wedged on a shelf for too long. Now then, what's your name?"

"Mr Happy," said Mr Happy, finding his voice at last.

"Hello, I'm a spell book," said the book. "I belong to a Wizard, but the silly, absent-minded fool left me here. Look! He even forgot his hat! When I was asleep someone tidied me away up on that shelf. I need a lift home. Will you help me?"

Mr Happy agreed, and wearing the Wizard's hat, with the spell book under his arm, he set off through the countryside.

Mr Happy felt just like a real Wizard!

Along the way they met Mr Forgetful who was standing beside a phone box muttering to himself.

"Do you have any spells in there that could help Mr Forgetful's memory?" Mr Happy asked the spell book.

"Of course," said the spell book, and opened on the right page.

Mr Happy read out the spell and watched Mr Forgetful.

"I remember!" cried Mr Forgetful. "I've got to ring Mr Chatterbox … and I forgot to lock my house … oh no, I forgot to turn off my bath … and I didn't post that letter … and I haven't bought any milk … and I must water the plants and …"

Mr Forgetful was frantically running around in circles by this point, worrying about all the things he had forgotten.

"Oh dear! Do you have any spells to make people forget things?" Mr Happy said to the book.

The spell book opened at a different page and as soon as Mr Happy said the spell, Mr Forgetful looked a lot happier.

Mr Happy and the spell book continued on their way.

They heard somebody talking to himself around a bend in the road.

"If I cross over now then I might get run over, but if I don't cross over then how will I get to the other side? Oh dear, oh dear."

It was Mr Worry.

Mr Happy looked down at the spell book.

"Do you want to know if I have any spells to stop people worrying?" guessed the spell book, and opened to the right page.

Mr Happy read out the spell.

"I don't care!" shouted Mr Worry, suddenly. "Hee! Hee! I'm worry free! I'll just close my eyes and step out into the …"

CRASH! He walked straight into Mr Bump on his bicycle.

"Maybe worrying is safer after all," said Mr Happy, and the spell book flicked over a couple of pages to the spell that would return Mr Worry to normal.

It was a very long walk to the Wizard's house. In the middle of the afternoon Mr Happy caught up with a hot and tired Mr Small.

"How about a spell for longer legs?" suggested Mr Happy.

"Coming right up," replied the spell book.

Mr Small's legs grew and grew.

He strode off down the road at a terrific pace, until he reached a tree and banged his head on a branch. The same thing happened on the second tree he came to. And on the trees all the way down the road.

BANG! OUCH!
BANG! OUCH!
BANG! OUCH!

Mr Happy winced.

"Shorter legs?" asked the spell book.

Mr Happy nodded.

By the evening they came to a wood.

"We're nearly there now," said the spell book happily.

Finally they reached a cottage in a clearing.

The Wizard opened the door. He was overjoyed.

"My spell book and my hat! I've been looking high and low for them for so long that I'd nearly given up hope! Thank you!"

He invited Mr Happy in for supper.

A Wizard's supper.

They ate Everything Pie.

The pie changed as they ate, so every mouthful tasted different!

After supper was finished and the washing-up spell had done its work, the Wizard turned to Mr Happy.

"There must be something I can do for you. Choose any spell you wish. Choose anything you want!"

Mr Happy smiled. "After seeing what spells can do, I think I'm happy as I am!" he laughed.